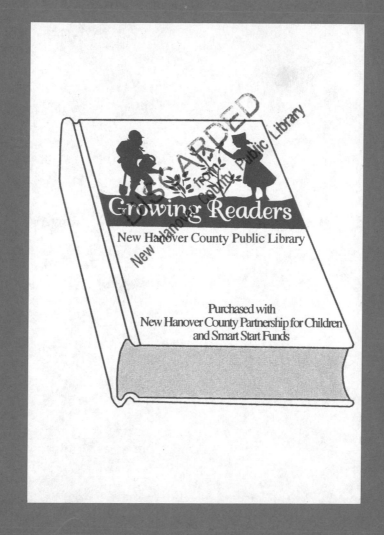

Stay Awake, Bear!

by GAVIN BISHOP

ORCHARD BOOKS • NEW YORK

Thank you, Ann—G.B.

Orchard Books, A Grolier Company
95 Madison Avenue, New York, NY 10016

Manufactured in the United States of America
Printed and bound by Phoenix Color Corp.
Book design by Mina Greenstein
The text of this book is set in 16 point Cheltenham Book.
The illustrations are watercolor with pen and ink.

10 9 8 7 6 5 4 3 2 1

Library of Congress Cataloging-in-Publication Data
Bishop, Gavin, date.
Stay awake, Bear! / by Gavin Bishop.   p.   cm.
Summary: Old Bear and his friend Brown Bear decide that
sleeping all winter is a waste of time, so they stay awake
planning a warm summer vacation and then sleep through
the whole trip.
ISBN 0-531-30249-0 (trade : alk. paper).—
ISBN 0-531-33249-7 (library bdg. : alk. paper)
[1. Bears Fiction. 2. Sleep Fiction.]   I. Title.
PZ7.B5254St 2000
[E]—dc21 99-29514

"**S**leeping is such a waste of time! It takes up the whole winter," said Old Bear as he watched the leaves turn yellow.

While the days shortened, Old Bear grumbled, "I don't want to go to sleep! I feel wide awake!"

But when the first snowflakes fell, he began to yawn. He turned up the radio to keep himself awake.

"This year," he said, "I am not going to fall asleep."

He watched his neighbors closing shutters and putting things away for the cold months ahead.

"Good-night, old friend," they called to him. "See you in the spring."

The snow fell thick and fast. Old Bear watched as the neighborhood houses grew dark and quiet under a great white blanket of snow.

Old Bear yawned a huge yawn. "I am *not* going to go to sleep," he said.

He kept busy. He filled his
days by playing songs on his
banjo. He sang along at the top
of his voice.

He baked pies and made spicy jam tarts.

And in the evenings he watched videos and read travel books.

After a time his yawning stopped.

He didn't feel tired anymore, not one little bit. "This is much better than sleeping away the winter!" he exclaimed.

But after a few months of reading, eating, and watching endless videos, Old Bear was restless.

Suddenly he heard a knock at the door.

He opened it and there, standing waist deep in the snow, was Brown Bear from the house next door.

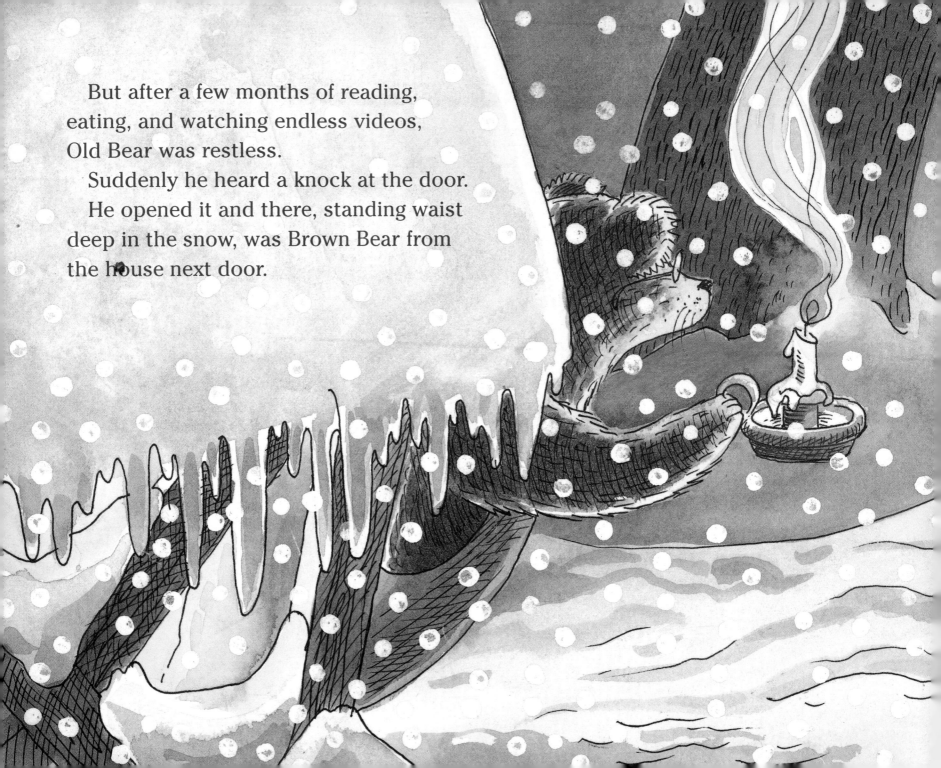

"I couldn't sleep," he said. "I just lay there thinking what a waste of time sleeping is. Then I saw your light."

So together the two bears stayed awake for the rest of the winter.

They played Scrabble every day.

They ate macaroni and cheese.

They planned a vacation for the warm sunny months ahead.

And when the days lengthened and the snow melted, they packed their bags and set off.

But by the time they reached the railway station, they were both yawning.

On the train the two bears fell into a deep sleep.

They snoozed along the seacoast,

slumbered through the mountains,

and snored crossing the plains.

At the end of their vacation, Old Bear and Brown Bear woke up.

"What a refreshing holiday that was," they both said. "What sights! What memories!"

They arrived home as the first snowflakes of winter began to fall.

"Do you feel tired?" asked Old Bear.

"I am as fresh as a daisy," said Brown Bear.

"Do you want to spend the winter sleeping?"

"No siree! Let's watch a movie."

"Good idea," said Old Bear. "Sleeping is such a waste of time!"

From that day on, the two bears
never again slept the winter away.
While their neighbors dozed,
Old Bear and Brown Bear
stayed awake.

They did jigsaw puzzles.

They ate pancakes with
honey.

And they dreamed of the wonderful vacation
they would have when the snow melted.
Zzzzzzzzzzz. . . .